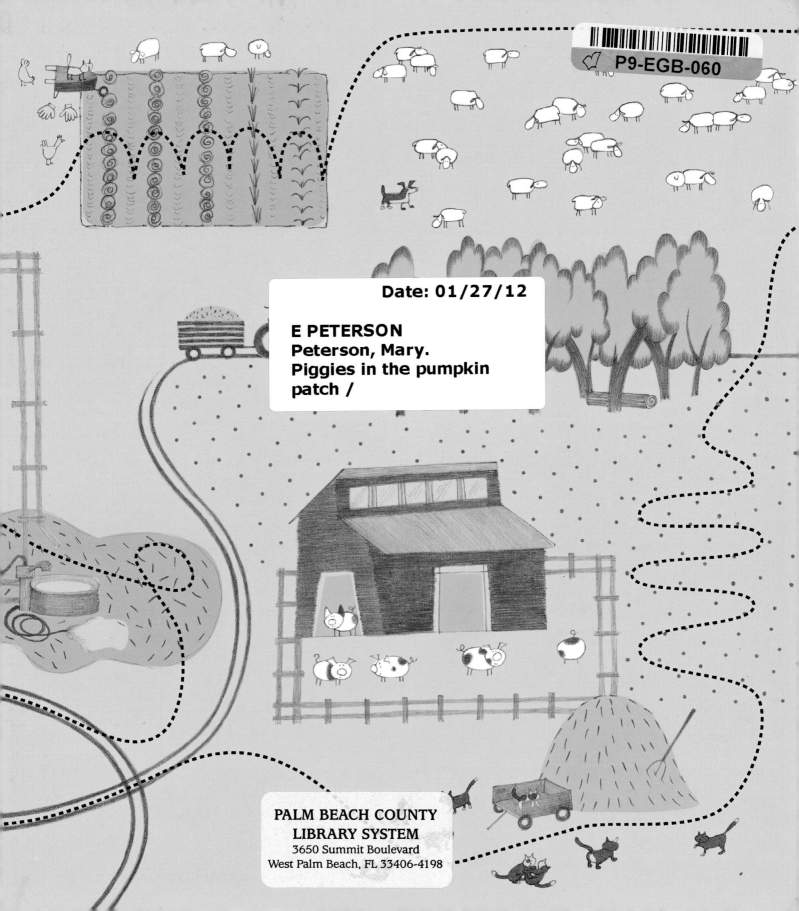

PIGGIES
in the
Pumpkin Patch

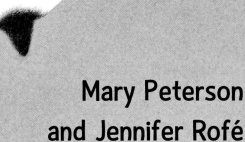

Mary Peterson
and Jennifer Rofé

ini Charlesbridge

Piggies in the pumpkin patch

peek

and sneak,

under crinkly,
clean sheets,

over growing, green beans,

behind snoring, sleepy sheep,

into the clover field.

Piggies in the clover field

chase

and race,

between teasing tabby cats,

along winding wagon tracks,

across muddy, matted grass,

into the big bull's pen.

Piggies in the
big bull's pen

crash

and dash,

through scrambling, shrieking geese,

past swarming, stinging bees,

into the pumpkin patch.

Piggies in the pumpkin patch,

deep asleep.

In memory of the farm on Grundy Road—M. P.

For Brady—J. R.

Published by Charlesbridge
85 Main Street
Watertown, MA 02472
(617) 926-0329
www.charlesbridge.com

Library of Congress Cataloging-in-Publication Data
Peterson, Mary.
Piggies in the pumpkin patch / Mary Peterson and Jennifer Rofé ;
illustrated by Mary Peterson.
p. cm.
Summary: Pigs have a wonderful time playing
in the pumpkin patch and other spots on the farm,
encountering other animals along the way.
ISBN 978-1-57091-460-7 (reinforced for library use)
ISBN 978-1-57091-461-4 (softcover)
[1. Pigs—Fiction. 2. Domestic animals—Fiction. 3. Farm life—Fiction.]
I. Rofé, Jennifer. II. Title.
PZ7.P44516Pig 2010
[E]—dc22   2009026652

Printed in China
(hc) 10 9 8 7 6 5 4 3 2
(sc) 10 9 8 7 6 5 4 3 2

Illustrations done in pencil and painted
in Adobe Photoshop and Adobe Illustrator
Display type and text type set in Humper by Typotheticals
Color separations by Chroma Graphics, Singapore
Printed and bound November 2010 by Yangjiang Millenium Litho Limited
in Yangjiang, Guangdong, China
Production supervision by Brian G. Walker
Designed by Martha MacLeod Sikkema

FINISH

START